PUFFIN BOO

CARROT TOPS

'Does a duck know it's a duck?' Calvin asked his mother the day they went in the bus to Kew Gardens.

'I'm not sure,' said his mother. 'They do know their friends.'

'Yes,' said Calvin, 'but when a duck sees itself in the water does it think "That's me"?'

All Calvin's mother could answer again to that was, 'I don't know,' but it *was* a good question, and only one of the fascinating thoughts that arise in these fifteen stories about young children enjoying their daily round of bus trips, visits to the supermarket, or the deserted beach, or making a jelly or paper dolls at home.

The children in this book are endlessly curious, ready to discuss every tiny thing they notice, and then to toss their new ideas around and try them in conversation and play with them every way until they have extracted every bit of interest and imagination from them.

Joan Wyatt is a writer with an unusually observant understanding of the processes of young children's thought and their thirst for conversation, and the result is a book that young listeners will instantly take to, and one that will set their parents thinking too.

Joan Wyatt was born in 1934 in Anglesey and educated in Shrewsbury and at Bedford College, London. She lived and taught in Maryland, USA, then in Leeds and Washington, D.C. She is married to a biologist and has two sons. Several of her stories were broadcast on the BBC.

JOAN WYATT

CARROT
TOPS

Stories for
Very Young Children

Illustrated by
Margery Gill

PUFFIN BOOKS

Puffin Books, Penguin Books Ltd, Harmondsworth, Middlesex, England
Viking Penguin Inc., 40 West 23rd Street, New York, New York 10010, U.S.A.
Penguin Books Australia Ltd, Ringwood, Victoria, Australia
Penguin Books Canada Limited, 2801 John Street, Markham, Ontario, Canada L3R 1B4
Penguin Books (N.Z.) Ltd, 182–190 Wairau Road, Auckland 10, New Zealand

—

First published by William Heinemann Ltd 1976
Published in Puffin Books 1978
Reprinted 1987

—

—

Made and printed in Great Britain
by Richard Clay (The Chaucer Press) Ltd,
Bungay, Suffolk
Set in Monotype Ehrhardt

Contents

For my parents

Cooking Day

Clive and his mother were cooking and talking. That was one of the good things about cooking, you could talk at the same time. (Not, of course, when everything was ready and you had to get out of the way because it was hot.) They were remembering the day at the seaside – and making apple pie at the same time. Every now and then Clive's mother gave him a slice of raw cooking apple. It was sour and made his mouth feel funny, but he liked it. Then there was the pastry. Clive wasn't that good at the rolling part, but he was jolly good at cutting out circles with the wavy cutters. He liked putting dabs of milk on scones too. He did quite a lot of cooking one way and another.

That day they remembered the sea – all blue like the sky. Clive had paddled and sailed his plastic boats. The sea wasn't blue where it splashed over his toes, just ordinary, no colour water – but far away it looked blue.

'Can we have blue jelly on Saturday?' asked Clive.

'Well, no,' said his mother. 'We could have red or orange or yellow or purple – but not blue, I'm afraid.'

'Why not?' said Clive. 'I like blue.'

'I don't know why, but people don't make blue jellies. We could try a blue cake one day if you like.'

'Let's have a green jelly then,' said Clive.

His mother gave him the packet to open and he looked at the pictures of jellies on the front. There weren't any blue ones but there were some lovely shapes, like sandcastles, well, sand pies, but shining and smooth.

Clive poured the runny jelly into a mould. He wanted to make his jelly just as beautiful as the ones on the packet. Then he put it to set, very carefully. Spilt jelly is so sticky, he knew from experience. Then he went off to play. A watched jelly never sets – or anyway it takes a very long time indeed.

On Saturday morning he looked at the green jelly. It was set quite firm.

'Can I turn it out?' he asked.

'Shall I do it? It's quite difficult,' said his mother.

'No, I want to do it all by myself,' said Clive and went for a plate.

Then he turned the jelly upside down, very, very, carefully. There was a lovely slurping noise and Clive knew the jelly had come out of the mould and on to the plate. But oh dear – only half the jelly was out; the rest of it was still stuck inside the mould. Clive felt angry and sad at the same time.

His jelly was all messy. It was no good. His mother tried to cheer him up.

'When I was a little girl we used to say,

> Wiggle, Waggle, Wiggle, Waggle,
> Jelly on the plate,

when we were skipping with a rope.'

But Clive didn't want to be cheered up. He wanted his jelly to look beautiful.

'Could you fetch your very small plastic boat from the bathroom?' said his mother.

'All right,' said Clive, but he wondered what she was up to.

When he came back his mother had put a big blue plate on the table.

'Now,' she said, 'if you chop your jelly up in little pieces, it will look like waves and you can sail your boat on it.'

Clive chopped away and the green jelly sparkled on the blue plate. He put his little boat to sail on the jelly sea, and it looked lovely.

'They should have pictures of boats on jelly packets,' said Clive and he licked the sail carefully.

Kew Gardens

Calvin woke early.

'Kew Day,' he said and stretched.

He meant it was the day for going to the gardens at Kew.

'We may have to queue for a bus,' he said and his mother laughed.

'Have I been there before?' said Calvin.

'Yes,' said his mother, 'but you were very little. You liked the grass and you liked the ducks, but I don't expect you remember.'

'I don't remember things now,' said Calvin. 'I can't remember which shoe.'

'Don't worry,' said his mother. 'You'll know if your foot feels squashed and you'll soon be able to tell from the outside. I'll help you in a minute.'

Calvin sat down and crossed his legs while he waited. His mother finished brushing her hair, then she put his shoes on for him. Calvin uncrossed his legs and stood up.

'Hey,' he said, 'they're on the wrong feet.'

'Well, they looked all right when I put them on,' said his mother. 'You'll have to jump with your feet crossed.'

'All the way to the bus?' said Calvin.

'Not really,' said his mother. 'Keep still.'

Then she changed his shoes over quickly.

'Why aren't feet the same both sides?' said Calvin.

'I don't know,' said his mother. 'Hands aren't either.'

'And only one nose,' said Calvin.

'Have you got your clean handkerchief?' said his mother.

'Yes,' said Calvin, 'but I forgot my other nose.'

They caught the bus for Kew.

'I wish it was a garden bus,' said Calvin, 'with window boxes. The conductor could water the flowers when he went upstairs for the fares.'

'Yes,' said his mother, 'and he could lean out and water the bus queue if the people looked all hot and cross.'

'They wouldn't look cross going to Kew,' said Calvin.

'No,' said his mother. 'You're right.'

Calvin watched all the people hurrying in the

street. He looked at the children out shopping with their mums and dads.

'Do you remember when I got lost?' he said.

'I do,' said his mother, 'the day you went back for your hat. But you were very clever, waiting in the shop for me to come and find you.'

'You took a long time,' said Calvin.

'Only a minute,' said his mother, 'but it seemed ages to me too.'

'I'm glad I found my hat,' said Calvin.

'So am I,' said his mother. She looked down at his red hat. 'I'm glad I found you both,' she said.

At last the conductor said, 'Kew Gardens,' and Calvin and his mother got off the bus and walked to the iron gates.

'I like gates you can see through,' said Calvin, but they didn't go in at the big gates. They walked to a fence with a kind of giant mincing machine in a gap.

'What's that?' said Calvin.

'It's a turnstile,' said his mother. 'It counts all the people who go in.'

Calvin was a bit doubtful.

'And come out?' he said.

'No,' said his mother, 'but it's all right. Hold my hand and we'll go through.'

14

The turnstile turned and it didn't hurt at all. Calvin and his mother were inside the gardens.

'Two more people,' said Calvin, 'but it doesn't know I'm me.'

'I do,' said his mother. 'Look at the ducks.'

Calvin looked at a drake with a dark green head and a bright brown tummy.

'They don't talk much,' he said. 'Does a duck know it's a duck?'

'I'm not sure,' said his mother. 'They do know their friends.'

'Yes,' said Calvin, 'but when a duck sees itself in the water, does it think "That's me"?'

'I don't know,' said his mother, 'but I'm sure they know their families.'

Calvin and his mother walked across the grass, then Calvin hid behind a tree and jumped out at his mother.

'Boo,' he said.

'I'm not a goose,' she said, 'and mind the ducks. They don't like boys jumping out at them.'

'Or girls,' said Calvin.

'No,' said his mother. 'Nor girls. One heavy foot feels just like another.'

'I wouldn't hurt them on purpose,' said Calvin.

'The ducks wouldn't know,' said his mother. 'And if you bumped into a swan he'd bump you back.'

Calvin was interested.

'Would he?' he said. 'With his foot?'

'No,' said his mother, 'with his wing.'

'Or hers,' said Calvin.

'Yes,' said his mother, 'or hers, especially if you went near her babies.'

'I'll be careful,' said Calvin and they walked along the path near the river.

'Look,' said Calvin and they watched two big swans swimming slowly. Behind them, politely, came their four grey little ones.

'The baby ones are called cygnets,' said Calvin's mother.

'Cygnets,' said Calvin. 'Aren't they fluffy?'

'They're wearing grey sweaters,' said his mother.

'Their mother never says, "Don't get wet," ' said Calvin.

'Perhaps,' said his mother, 'perhaps she says, "Don't get dry."'

Then Calvin and his mother turned away from the swans and came to the 'inside' garden.

Calvin didn't remember the 'inside' garden at

all. When the heavy door shut you were inside a great glass house, all hot and steamy. There wasn't any grass, but there were trees, really big ones, not little ones in pots. Calvin looked at the trees.

'Aren't they too hot?' he said.

'No,' said his mother. 'They like it. Would you like to take your coat off?'

'Yes,' said Calvin and he took off his coat and his hat.

His mother took her coat off too.

'I'm still hot,' said Calvin.

'Take your sweater off then,' said his mother. 'I'll hold your coat.'

Calvin pulled his grey sweater off over his head.

'Can I take my socks off?' he said.

'I wouldn't,' said his mother. 'You might lose them. We won't stay in here long.'

'All right,' said Calvin.

He was carrying his hat and his coat, his mittens were in the pockets and he'd tied his sweater round his waist by the sleeves.

'You look like an explorer,' said his mother.

'I'm looking for the way out,' said Calvin.

'I'd like to see the upside down tree,' said his mother.

'They all look the right way up to me,' said Calvin. 'Can we go now? I'm hot.'

'Just a minute,' said his mother.

'Can I take my vest off?' said Calvin.

'No,' said his mother. 'Come on, we may see my tree on the way out, or perhaps we can come another day.'

'Let's choose a cold day then,' said Calvin.

'It *is* cold outside,' said his mother. 'We'll have to get dressed again.'

'Look,' said Calvin, 'sparrows, ordinary sparrows.'

'I expect they came in for a warm,' said his mother.

Calvin found a feather on the slatted wooden path.

'Well,' he said, 'this sparrow was too hot.' Then he put the feather in his pocket to take home.

'I wonder if it's a vest feather or a sock feather,' he said.

'I don't think sparrows have feathery feet,' said his mother.

'I'll look,' said Calvin.

At last they gave up looking for the upside down tree and came out of the hot house. The air was cool on their faces. Calvin turned to watch four baby swans.

'Cigarettes,' he said.

'Where?' said his mother.

'There,' said Calvin, 'without their mother.'

'Oh yes,' said his mother, 'cygnets. I wonder where their mother's gone. They look a bit worried.'

'Shall we catch them,' said Calvin, 'and take them to their mother?'

'No,' said his mother, 'I expect she'll come and find them in a minute. Let's wait and see.'

Calvin and his mother stood quite still and waited. They watched the cygnets walking up and down. Then they watched them running up and down.

'Their feet flap,' said Calvin.

'They are anxious,' said his mother. 'I hope their mother comes soon.'

Then round the corner of the bushes came two great swans and the cygnets ran towards them.

'Oh,' said Calvin. 'Black swans. I didn't know about black swans.'

Calvin and his mother watched the big swans and their cygnets walk down to the water and swim away.

'I wish I could swim,' said Calvin.

'You will,' said his mother. 'You soon will. I expect you'll be a good swimmer.'

'Like a swan?' said Calvin.

'Well, more like a puppy at first,' said his mother. 'More splashy, but just as nice.'

'Can you swim?' said Calvin.

'Yes,' said his mother, 'but not like a swan.'

Big Shop, Little Shop

Jean liked shopping in the shining big supermarket round the corner.

'Can I push the trolley?' she said.

'Yes,' said her mother, 'if there aren't too many people.'

'I'll mind the baked beans this time,' said Jean and she steered very carefully.

'Cornflakes,' said her mother.

'I know,' said Jean, and off they went down one long row and up the next, taking tins and packets from the shelves. Then they paid for their shopping on the way out.

One fine day Jean's mother was carrying a suitcase instead of a shopping bag and they walked right past the supermarket. They weren't going shopping. They were going to catch a train to see Jean's Granny and Grandad in the country. You had to ask the guard to stop the train especially for

you because there wasn't a proper railway station,
only a name and a little platform.

'Do you think the guard will remember?' said
Jean.

'He always does,' said her mother, and the train
stopped.

Jean's Grandad came to meet them and her
Granny was waiting at home with the kettle on the
boil.

'Tea is ready,' said Jean's Granny and hugged

them both. Then she hugged Grandad too, in case he felt left out.

One day Jean and her mother walked to the village to buy bread and stamps. Jean watched the birds fly out of the hedge on either side.

'Do birds have holidays?' she said.

'Some of them do,' said her mother, 'well, they go on long journeys.'

'How do they know where to stop?' said Jean.

'I don't know,' said her mother, 'but they do.'

'I know where the shop is,' said Jean and the bell on the door rang as they went in.

'Fee, fo, fi, fum,' said Jean quietly, 'I smell apples and candles, cheese and dog biscuits.' She sniffed. 'Bread and soap. Ooh,' she said loudly, 'this shop does smell.'

Mrs Jones the shopkeeper looked hurt and the other customers looked surprised.

'I think Jean means that the shop smells interesting,' said her mother.

'Yes,' said Jean, 'the supermarket doesn't smell.'

'Interesting,' said her mother.

Jean looked at all the things that didn't smell: light bulbs, tins of spaghetti, string.

'Ooh,' she said, 'this is a lovely shop.'

Mrs Jones looked more cheerful and went on serving her customers. People waited their turn in this shop: they didn't pick things up and put them in their baskets.

'Can I help you?' said Mrs Jones at last.

'Yes please,' said Jean's mother, 'we'd like a large white loaf.'

Mrs Jones put the bread on the counter.

'Will that be all?' she said.

'No,' said Jean's mother, 'we'd like ten stamps, please.'

Jean had been surprised the first time they bought stamps in the shop, but now she knew what to do. Mrs Jones walked round the back of the counter and Jean and her mother met her at the other end of the shop: that end of the shop was the post office. Mrs Jones stood behind the wire. Like a hen, thought Jean, but she didn't say so. Jean looked at the big scales for weighing parcels and the small scales for weighing letters.

'I could play post-office-shop,' she said when she got home.

Granny gave her a big piece of paper and Grandad ruled squares on it. Then Jean drew tiny pictures in all the squares and pricked round them with a pin.

'Look at my stamps,' she said, 'they tear off like grown-up ones.'

Then she crayoned a pile of pound notes.

'You're very rich,' said Granny.

'It's post office money,' said Jean, and borrowed some little buttons for change.

'Don't lose them,' said Granny, 'your Grandad's a great man for bursting his buttons.'

Jean borrowed the scales from the kitchen. She had to be careful with the heavy weights, but she liked making the scales balance.

At teatime Jean weighed tea, sugar, butter and jam, and they began the new loaf.

'Crust or crumb?' said Grandad.

That meant, 'Would you like the outside crust or an inside piece?'

'Crumb, please,' said Jean.

'Crust, please,' said her mother.

When Jean gave the buttons back at bedtime she said, 'Can I borrow the scales and the buttons next time, please?'

'Of course you can,' said Granny, 'and I'll buy some more stamps.'

The next day the guard stopped the train for Jean and her mother to get on. They waved good-bye and in no time at all they were home. They unpacked the fresh eggs Granny had given them. They unpacked their suitcase, but Jean couldn't find any home-made money or stamps.

'I must have left them on the scales,' she said.

The next morning their postman, a friendly man who thumped his heels hard on the pavement, brought Jean a fat letter.

'You're in luck,' he said.

'Thank you,' said Jean and opened the fat letter. Inside was another envelope with one of her stamps in the corner.

'Dear Jean,' said the letter,
'We found your stamps and your money as soon as you had gone. Here they are post haste. Do send us a picture of your post office if you have time.
Love from
Granny and Grandad.'

Jean sat down right away and drew a picture with scales and chicken wire.

'I haven't got the chicken wire, really,' she said, 'but it's nice to draw.'

'It makes your picture look very post office,' said her mother. 'Are you going to work in a post office when you grow up?'

'I might,' said Jean, 'but a shop might smell more.'

'Interesting,' said her mother.

Paper Men

Steve and his mother walked home through the shopping centre. The shops were ordinary, but there was a roof over the street and there weren't any cars. People could sit down on long seats and children could run about.

'Look,' said Steve's mother, 'there's someone like Big Granny.'

'Not very like,' said Steve, 'her coat's different.' He looked down. 'The same kind of shoes though,' he said.

They stopped for a moment outside the television shop. The big windows were full of television sets – some coloured and some black and white. Steve remembered something.

'What's "portable"?' he said.

'It's something you can carry,' said his mother, 'a little television.'

'Oh,' said Steve, 'like babies. Babies are portable and big boys aren't.'

'Well, not for long,' said his mother.

They looked at the television sets. On each screen there was a man talking.

'What's he talking about?' said Steve.

'I don't know,' said his mother. 'We might guess if we could stay, but we must go home now.'

The television man waved; the man on all the other sets waved at exactly the same moment.

'They're saying good-bye,' said Steve, and he waved back.

The special doors opened by themselves for Steve and his mother to walk out of the shopping centre.

'It's funny there's only one me,' said Steve.

'And one me,' said his mother.

'But two grannies,' said Steve.

'Well, they're not the same,' said his mother. 'One's big and one's little and they're different inside.'

'Big Granny showed me a new thing,' said Steve. 'I'll show you when we get home.'

After tea Steve's mother gave him a piece of paper and he drew round a plate.

'It has to be a clean plate,' he said. 'No jam.'

Then he found his cutting-out scissors.

'Even scissors are different,' he said. 'Mine are round and yours are pointed.'

He cut carefully round the line and then he had a paper circle.

'Is that the new thing?' said his mother.

'Not yet,' said Steve.

He folded the circle in half, then in half again, then in half again until he had a pointed slice of paper cake.

'Is it to eat?' said his mother.

'No,' said Steve, 'it isn't finished yet. It's your turn now. Can you draw a man?'

Steve's mother drew a man on the top layer of folded paper.

32

'He has to keep his arms out,' said Steve, 'right out.'

'Like this?' said his mother.

Steve looked at the man standing with his legs apart and his arms out straight.

'Yes,' he said, 'he's like the man Big Granny drew. Now you cut him out. Mind you don't cut his arms off.'

It was quite hard to make the scissors cut

through so many layers of paper, but Steve's mother managed.

'There you are,' she said.

Steve looked at the top paper man with the other little men lined up behind.

'Now,' he said, and very gently he unfolded the paper. There stood all the men, holding hands in a circle.

'They're all the same,' said his mother.

'I'm going to make them different,' said Steve.

He crayoned the first man a smart row of buttons. The second had an extra big pocket. The third wore a red scarf.

'They're different,' said Steve, 'outside and in.'

'They're very thin,' said his mother. 'They can't have much inside. Would they like some tea?'

'I'll make them some,' said Steve and cut some tiny pieces of paper.

'They like biscuits,' he said.

'Ginger?' said his mother.

'Yes,' said Steve.

'Would you like a button for a plate?' said his mother.

'Yes please,' said Steve and he piled the paper biscuits on a blue button plate.

'Don't they like sandwiches?' said his mother.

'Not as much as biscuits,' said Steve, 'but I'll make them a few.'

He cut some tiny squares and put them on a yellow button plate.

'What's in the sandwiches?' said his mother.

'Paper jam,' said Steve, 'and paper peanut butter. You can't see inside them.'

'You can't see inside the people,' said his mother.

Steve's men ate all the biscuits and most of the sandwiches.

'What are they going to do now?' said his mother.

'Play "Ring o' Roses",' said Steve. 'They like that.'

So the men played 'Ring o' Roses' and they all said, 'Tishoo, tishoo, we all fall down.'

They played it three times, then Steve said, 'They're tired of that. What can they do now?'

He held his cutting-out scissors open then shut. 'Stiff legs,' he said, 'they can't run, but they can walk.'

Then he walked their round feet over to his circle of little men.

'I expect you're tired of holding hands,' he said and snipped the paper between the first paper man and the second.

'This man wants to go away and hide,' he said.

So Steve hid the first paper man, the one with the buttons.

'Where's he gone?' said the second.

'Do you want to look for him?' said Steve.

'Yes,' said the second paper man. 'I'll soon find him.'

And the second paper man, the one with the big pocket, set off in a hurry to look for the first.

'We want to go together,' said the next man, Red Scarf.

'Don't get lost,' said Steve.

'We won't,' they said. 'See you.'

'Is there a spare sandwich?' said a man with big teeth. 'I'm hungry.'

'Yes,' said Steve, 'peanut butter or jam?'

'Peanut butter, please,' said the man and he walked away chewing happily.

The next man was fidgeting and looking at his feet.

'My shoes are tight,' he said, 'they're pinching my toes.'

'All right,' said Steve, 'if you stand still, I'll crayon you some new ones.'

'Can I have boots instead?' said the man. 'Big ones?'

'Yes,' said Steve and crayoned a bit more.

'Thank you,' said the man. He stamped first one foot then the other. 'That's better,' he said.

The two men left behind were arguing.

'Sandwiches are silly,' said one.

'No, they're not,' said the other.

'Yes, they are.'

'No, they're not.'

'Do stop arguing,' said Steve. 'Why don't you play by yourselves until you feel friendly?'

The little paper men were quiet for a moment, then they began again, quietly at first, then loudly.

'He's not my friend,' said one.

'Yes, I am,' said the other.

'No, you're not.'

'Yes, I am.'

'Be quiet,' said Steve, 'I can't think straight.' Then he hid one cross man behind the curtain. The other scrambled down and sat under the table.

Steve's mother came into the room. She looked at the left-over scraps of paper.

'Where have all the men gone?' she asked.

'They were tired of being joined together,' said Steve. 'They went away to do things.'

Steve licked his finger and a tiny square of paper stuck to it.

'One of them,' he said, 'thought sandwiches were silly, so the others ate his.'

'I expect they'll be back later,' said Steve's mother, 'or tomorrow. Come and have your bath now.'

Steve liked baths.

'Paper men don't have baths,' he said.

'They use dry water,' said his mother. She turned on the taps and wet water gushed out. Steve was sitting in the bath playing with his red boat when he saw a flash of red on the taps. He waved his boat and from the taps two red boats waved back.

'Look,' he said. 'I'm twins, with two boats.'

He held his hands in front of his face and giant hands shone from the taps.

'Look how big my hands are,' he said. 'When will they stop growing?'

'When you're grown up,' said his mother.

'Why?' said Steve.

'Because you'll be big enough then,' said his mother.

'I'd like to see over people's heads,' said Steve.

'You did,' said his mother. 'When you sat on Daddy's shoulder and the Queen went by.'

'So I did,' said Steve. 'I had to hold tight.'

'The ground doesn't seem so far away,' said his mother, 'when you're standing on your own feet.'

'I crayoned one of the paper men some new shoes,' said Steve, 'boots, really. I'll make some red tarts tomorrow. I wish crayon jam was sticky.'

'Are you going to stick the men together again?'

said his mother. 'They're not like Humpty Dumpty.'

'I may,' said Steve. 'I'll see how they feel. They may want to play "Ring o' Roses", or they may not.'

'Can you remember where they all went?' said his mother.

'No,' said Steve, 'it'll be hide and seek. I'll have to find them.'

'Do you remember when you found that brussel sprout in your boot?' said his mother.

'Yes,' said Steve. 'And you found that old tea-bag in the teapot.'

'Yes,' said his mother. 'I thought it was a mouse and you laughed.'

'So did you,' said Steve. 'This bath's gone cold.'

He stood up suddenly and shivered. For a second he lost sight of his reflection in the taps.

'Where've I gone?' he said. 'Where's both of me?'

'I'll settle for one,' said his mother and held out the big towel.

'Please,' said Steve, 'I must find them.'

He bent to look for himself in the taps.

'Look!' he shouted.

'What?' said his mother. 'Don't splash.'

'Four,' he said, 'I counted four.'

'I'm glad only one splashes,' said his mother. 'Could you all get out now?'

'All right,' said Steve and he climbed out. 'I know where to look for me now.'

Lost – Found

Jenny was shopping with her mother in the super-market. They'd finished shopping really: they were waiting in the queue to pay. Jenny looked at the sweets on the low shelves.

'Can we?' she said.

'No,' said her mother, 'not today. We've bought biscuits already.'

Jenny watched the man in front put cornflakes and soup on the counter, on the black moving strip.

'It's nice ordinary shopping moves by itself,' she said, 'but cars would go better.'

Then Jenny looked up at the till. There on top was a small blue knitted shoe.

'Look,' said Jenny.

'It's very nicely knitted,' said her mother.

'Are they trying to sell it?' said Jenny.

'No,' said her mother, 'they've put it up there for people to see. Perhaps someone will come back for it.'

'It's a baby's,' said Jenny.

'Yes,' said her mother. 'I expect some baby kicked it off – you know how they do.'

Jenny thought. 'Yes,' she said. 'I know.' She thought again.

'It's funny when they drop things out of their prams,' she said, 'on purpose.'

'I remember when you did,' said her mother.

'A lot?' said Jenny.

'Yes,' said her mother, 'you were a good dropper. You thought it was very funny.'

At last it was their turn to pay; their biscuits and tins of beans and tomatoes and rice pudding moved along all by themselves on the black strip. Then Jenny's mother put them in her big shopping bag.

'Can I carry the biscuits?' said Jenny.

'Yes,' said her mother, 'but don't open the packet until we get home. I don't want you feeding any pigeons by mistake.'

'Can we feed them on purpose one day?' said Jenny.

'Yes,' said her mother, 'but not with biscuits.'

Outside it was just beginning to get cold.

'I expect that baby's got cold toes,' said Jenny.

'I expect he's been hiding them under his

43

blanket,' said her mother. 'You used to hide your face in your hands.'

'What did you say?' said Jenny.

'I said, "Where's Jenny?", then you'd jump up and shout, "Here I am." I was always surprised,' said her mother.

'Babies are funny,' said Jenny.

'Yes,' said her mother, 'funny, and a lot of the time they're nice.'

When they got home they unpacked the shopping. Jenny played shop with the tins.

'Did you see where I put my purse?' said her mother.

Jenny put down the tins of tomatoes.

'In your pocket,' she said. Then she found the beans and put them in front because she liked beans better than tomatoes. Then she picked up the rice pudding.

'Where's my purse gone now?' said her mother. 'It was here a second ago.'

Jenny put the rice pudding down and went to look for the purse.

She looked in all the usual places: in the shopping bag, under the newspaper, in the bathroom. Then she found it.

'Here it is,' she said.

'Where was it?' said her mother.

'At the bottom of the stairs,' said Jenny, 'it was a new place.'

'Thank you very much,' said her mother. 'I must have put it down for a second. You are good at finding things.'

45

Yes, thought Jenny, I know. Then she picked up the rice pudding.

The next day there was a grey sky and a cold wind.

'Shall I wear my new hat?' said Jenny.

'Yes,' said her mother, 'it's just the day for a new hat.'

'And new mittens,' said Jenny, and put her new hat on.

'I made the bobbles,' she said.

'Yes,' said her mother. 'They're good bobbles.'

But the mittens were even better. They didn't have any bobbles: they had faces instead. One mitten looked happy and the other looked sad. One woollen mouth turned up and the other turned down. Jenny's mittens talked to each other when she waggled her hands.

'Hello,' said the happy mitten.

'Oh dear,' said the sad one.

Jenny walked beside her mother and the mittens came along quietly. They all went into the post office and their queue moved more slowly than the others.

'Look at all the people,' said Jenny's happy mitten.

'Oh dear,' said the sad one.

'It's always like this,' said her mother.

'Everybody can't be in the slowest queue,' said Jenny.

'Well it feels like it,' said her mother. 'Now where's my purse?'

'With the yellow books,' said Jenny.

'Thank you,' said her mother.

After the post office, they went to the green-grocer.

47

'He's called the greengrocer,' said Jenny, 'because he sells cabbage.'

'He sells oranges,' said her mother, 'and potatoes. Why isn't he the orange and brown grocer?'

'I don't know,' said Jenny.

'Neither do I,' said her mother.

After the post office and the orange and brown greengrocer, they went to the supermarket. It wasn't very crowded so they walked quickly down the rows and paid for their shopping.

'There,' said Jenny's mother. 'That's done. We needn't go near a shop for days. Let's catch the bus home.'

While they were waiting for the bus, Jenny's mother looked at Jenny.

'You do look smart,' she said. 'Bobbles and all. Is your other mitten in your pocket?'

'No,' said Jenny. 'It isn't.'

She was wearing her sad mitten but there was only a hand at the end of her other sleeve.

'Oh dear,' said her mother, 'we'll have to go back and look for it. Now where did we go this morning?'

'The post office,' said Jenny, 'the orange and

48

brown greengrocer and the supermarket. But it's all right, I know where to look.'

'Where?' said her mother.

'In the supermarket,' said Jenny. 'I left him on the counter. I wanted them to put him on the till for everyone to see.'

'Oh dear,' said Jenny's mother. 'Well, at least we needn't trail back to the post office.'

'Or the orange and brown greengrocer,' said Jenny.

Back they went to the supermarket. Sure enough, there on the till sat Jenny's happy mitten.

'He's very nicely knitted,' said the shop lady, 'but I'm surprised he looks so cheerful.'

'Oh he's all right,' said Jenny. 'He knew I'd come back, but his friend was getting worried.'

'You're like Cinderella with her other slipper,' said the shop lady.

'More like a silly kitten who lost her mitten,' said Jenny's mother.

'I didn't really lose him,' said Jenny. 'I knew where he was all the time.' Jenny looked at her mother's big shopping bag.

'Have you got your purse?' she said.

Jenny's mother looked inside the bag.

'Yes,' she said, 'I really have.'

Then she thanked the shop lady for looking after Jenny's mitten.

'You're welcome,' said the shop lady. 'Good-bye.'

'Good-bye,' said the happy mitten and they went out to wait for the bus.

'The bus won't be long now,' said Jenny's mother.

Jenny's happy mitten smiled at his friend.

'Hello,' he said. 'I'm back.'

But the sad one frowned and shook his head, 'Oh dear,' he said. 'Oh dear.'

'Some mittens never change,' said Jenny's mother. Then the bus came.

Winter Sea

Andrew lived near the sea. He didn't go to the seaside for a day, or for a week. He lived all the year round in a house near the sea.

In the summer there were donkeys to ride on the beach and Punch and Judy to watch. Andrew stood with the other children and shouted back at Mr Punch.

'He isn't real,' said his mother afterwards.

'I know,' said Andrew, 'but he does make me jump. When I grow up I'm going to be a Punch and Judy man.'

Then he practised talking in a funny voice.

'Hello, children,' he said. 'I'm Mr Punch.'

But when winter came Andrew said in his ordinary voice, 'I like it when there's only us on the beach.'

'So do I,' said his mother. 'I miss the donkeys, but they'd be very cold waiting for people to have rides.'

'What do donkeys do in the winter?' said Andrew.

'I don't know,' said his mother. 'We'll have to ask the man next summer.'

Andrew and his mother walked near the sea. The wind blew cold in their faces and made their noses run.

'I know what an ice-cream feels like,' said Andrew, 'all cold inside.'

'Let's run,' said his mother and they thudded

along in their boots. First they ran against the wind, then they turned and let the wind push them.

'Have you found any treasures to take home?' said his mother.

'No,' said Andrew. 'I can't look properly. We're going too fast.'

When the wind dropped Andrew walked slowly, searching the sand for special stones and shells. He found three good stones: first a pure white one, then a black one, then a white one with a pink stripe. He felt them smooth and round in his pocket.

'Would you like a little plastic bag for your stones?' said his mother.

'Yes, please,' said Andrew and he put his three new stones in the bag. But whoosh, the wind snatched it out of his hand.

Andrew chased his treasure bag along the beach, off the wet sand on to the dry.

'Stop,' he shouted, 'wait for me,' but the bag went on.

'Wait,' he shouted. Then he caught it. 'What I need,' he said, 'is a heavy stone.'

Then he held the bag very tightly while he searched.

'There,' he said at last, 'that should help.'

He put the bag down on the sand in front of him.

'Keep still,' he said in his Mr Punch voice. 'Be good and keep still.'

And the bag kept almost still. The wind tugged, but the bag couldn't blow away because of the heavy stone.

Andrew looked up at the white foam far out on the grey sea.

'Soap,' he said, 'cold, cold soap. Does the sea freeze?'

He picked up his bag and walked over to the rocks.

'Can you slide on the rock pools?' he asked. 'Do the crabs skid on the ice?'

Then he tried to walk sideways like a crab, but crabs have more legs and no wellington boots.

'I think the sea is too salty to freeze,' said his mother.

'What about icebergs?' said Andrew.

'That's where it's really cold,' said his mother, 'where the polar bears live. You don't see many polar bears round here, do you?'

'I wish we did,' said Andrew. 'And my hands are cold enough.'

'Have you lost your mittens?' said his mother.

'No,' said Andrew. 'They're too clumsy for picking things up. Bare hands are better.'

'And colder,' said his mother.

'I don't mind,' said Andrew. Then he felt his stone bag and the piece of string handy in his pocket.

Andrew walked backwards so that the wind couldn't blow in his face.

'Where does the wind go?' he said. 'Does it pile up in a great whoosh or leak out round corners?'

'I think it's like you shouting,' said his mother. 'Where does your shout go when you stop?'

'Inside me,' said Andrew. 'Listen.'

Then he opened his mouth and out burst a great yell.

'Can you taste the salt on your lips?' said his mother.

'Yes,' shouted Andrew.

'You know potato crisps?' said his mother.

'Yes,' shouted Andrew.

'Well,' said his mother, 'they used to have a little blue paper bag of salt in every packet. But sometimes there were two blue bags by mistake, then you felt lucky.'

As they walked home along the sea front the wind tugged at their coats and their scarves flew like flags. Andrew's plastic bag was safe with the string in his pocket.

'I was lucky today,' he said. 'I found a good black stone, a good white stone and a stripy one like rock.'

'Like rock you eat?' said his mother.

'Yes,' said Andrew, 'but my stone has a stripe not writing and it isn't sticky.'

When they were home and warm, away from the wind, Andrew listened to the sound of the sea in his best pointed curly shell.

'It's funny,' he said. 'You can hear the sea inside, but you can't turn it up like television.'

'No,' said his mother. 'You have to turn yourself down to listen.'

Andrew listened to the shell sea again. Then he had an idea.

'Can I borrow your little mirror?' he said.

'Yes,' said his mother, 'but be careful because it might break.'

So Andrew was careful. He arranged his stones, old ones and new around the mirror.

'Look,' he said. 'Look at my rock pool, my frozen sea.'

Then he took out his polar bear.

'That's where you live,' he said.

And the bear looked at himself in the ice-mirror.

'He's a bit lonely,' said Andrew. 'Who else lives on the ice?'

'Seals do,' said his mother.

'Oink, oink,' said Andrew.

'And penguins,' said his mother, 'but you haven't got any. Why don't you let the other animals come for the day? They'd like that.'

'Yes,' said Andrew and he marched all his animals out of their box.

'Ducks have short legs,' he said, 'I'll put them on the new big stone. They'll see better from there.'

He looked at the other animals standing in line.

'It's all right for the lion,' he said, 'with his fur collar, but the ostrich looks cold.'

'Yes,' said his mother. 'Those long bare legs. Perhaps he's growing out of his feathers. I expect he'll be glad to get home.'

'He could wear socks,' said Andrew. 'Dogs wear coats sometimes. I've seen them.'

Andrew looked at his frozen sea, then he looked at the icicles on the drain-pipe outside.

'I'm glad we don't eat our fish fingers frozen,' he said.

'Wouldn't you like a fish lolly?' said his mother. 'With tomato sauce?'

'No, thank you,' said Andrew. 'Nor fish jelly and custard.'

'What about fish trifle and baked beans?' said his mother.

'Yes please,' said Andrew. 'I'd like baked beans.'

So they made some toast and didn't let it burn, then they ate it all hot with the beans. Then Andrew walked his animals home to their box, and his mother took back her mirror.

'The ice has melted,' she said. 'Time for bed.'

'I'll put my stones away,' said Andrew, 'but I'll take my curly shell to bed with me.'

'For going to sleep?' said his mother.

'Yes,' said Andrew, 'like your clock for waking up.'

'All right,' said his mother, 'but it'll be bumpy to lie on.'

'I'll put it in my pyjama pocket,' said Andrew. 'Why don't animals have pockets for things?'

'Perhaps they remember them instead,' said his mother.

Halfway upstairs Andrew stopped.

'Kangaroos do,' he said.

'What?' said his mother.

'Have pockets,' said Andrew.

'Only for baby kangaroos,' said his mother.

'Is that all?' said Andrew. 'No shells or string?'

'No,' said his mother and opened the bedroom door.

Andrew got into bed.

'Tomorrow,' he said, 'I'll take the animals to my sea again. Not the ostrich though, unless he wears socks.'

He listened to his curly shell.

'I could wind string round his legs,' he said, 'but wool might be warmer. Did you see how fast I ran after my bag?'

'Yes,' said his mother.

'You know,' said Andrew. 'I can remember things and I can bring them home in my pockets.'

'Yes,' said his mother. 'You're lucky.'

'Good night,' said Andrew in his Mr Punch voice.

'Good night, Mr Punch,' said his mother. Then she went downstairs.

One Potato, Two Potato

Tom helped his mother scrub the potatoes. He looked at the water, dark in the bowl.

'Mud soup,' he said. 'Why doesn't it taste nice?'

'I don't know,' said his mother, 'but the potatoes will. I'll just put them in the oven, then we can go.'

'They'll be waiting for us when we come home,' said Tom. 'We'll smell them.'

Tom and his mother went out to wait for the bus to his Granny's.

'Perhaps the empty matchboxes will be there today,' said Tom, 'Granny's been collecting them for ages.'

'Perhaps Mr Jones next door has given her some,' said Tom's mother. 'His pipe is always going out, so he must use lots of matches.'

'I wish Granny smoked a pipe,' said Tom.

'Why?' said his mother.

'I could borrow it for a snowman,' said Tom.

'But there isn't any snow,' said his mother.

'I'll wait,' said Tom, and the bus came.

It was only a short way on the bus, then they walked together to Granny's. Tom opened the gate while his mother hurried off to work. Just before the corner she turned to wave and Tom waved back. Then he ran round to his Granny's back door and his feet crunched on the gravel. The front door handle was too high, but he could open the back door easily.

Tom walked into his Granny's kitchen.

'Hello,' said his Granny, 'I've been waiting for you.'

'Hello,' said Tom, 'we had to wait for the bus this morning. Have you got the matchboxes?'

'Yes,' said his Granny, and Tom saw the big brown carrier bag on the table.

'Mrs Jones gave me some,' said Granny. 'You can take them home with you. What are you going to make?'

'I don't know yet,' said Tom. 'I haven't decided. I'll tell you next week.'

Then Tom and his Granny did some jobs. Tom dried the spoons and the plastic dishes while his Granny did some ironing.

Sometimes they talked and sometimes they didn't. Then Granny sang,

> 'This is the way I iron the clothes,
> Iron the clothes, iron the clothes,'

and Tom sang,

> 'On a cold and frosty morning.'

Then Tom sang,

> 'This is the way I dry the spoons,
> Dry the spoons, dry the spoons,'

and his Granny joined in,

> 'On a cold and frosty morning.'

'It isn't very cold and frosty,' said Tom. 'Can we go for a walk?'

'Yes,' said his Granny, 'I'd like that. Just let me finish this ironing.'

Tom looked at the iron.

'It's a small steam roller,' he said.

He liked watching the clothes go smooth and he liked the warm ironing smell, but he did wish his Granny would hurry up. He put on his coat and his boots and his mittens.

'Can we go now?' he said and turned the door knob.

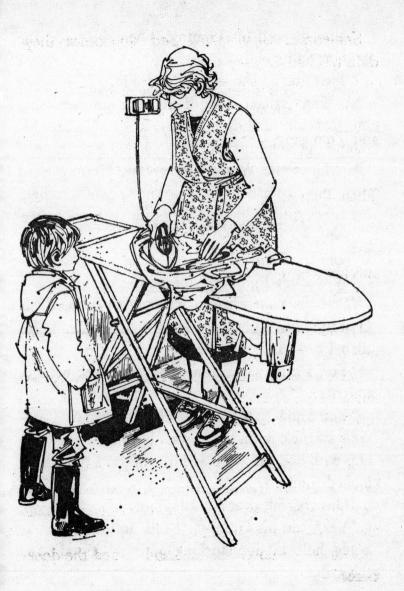

'Almost,' said his Granny. Then she stood the iron up on its end.

'There now,' she said, 'I'm ready.'

As they walked along Tom sang another song, but this time he didn't sing the words. He kept his mouth open and patted it while he sang the tune of 'Pop Goes the Weasel'. Then his Granny went POP, not like a balloon, you know. She just held her cheek stiff and pinged the inside with one finger.

POP.

Tom tried and tried.

'Why can't I go pop?' he said.

'Perhaps your cheek isn't tough yet,' said his Granny, 'but you can run upstairs much faster than I can. And you can skip.'

'Yes, I can,' said Tom, 'and my cheek will get tougher.'

'You know,' said Tom's Granny, 'when I was your size, I couldn't skip with both feet. I used to hop with one and walk with the other. I must have looked funny.'

'Did you fall over?' said Tom.

'Yes,' said his Granny, 'I did, and once I made a big hole in my stocking and my leg showed through.'

'Girls wear tights now,' said Tom.

'Yes,' said his Granny, 'but we didn't then.'

Tom skipped a little way ahead then he skipped all round his Granny.

'You're a sheep dog rounding me up,' she said. 'Mind I don't trip over you. I don't want another hole in my stocking.'

All the way home Tom and his Granny played sheep dogs. His Granny whistled: once for stop and twice for go.

'What does "pop" mean?' said Tom.

'It means "mind that puddle",' said his Granny.

'No,' said Tom, 'that's PLOP.'

'When I lived near a pond,' said his Granny, 'we used to hear the frogs plopping into the water one after each other. Plop, plop, plop, plop. It was like a race, but they didn't start off together.'

'Ready, steady, go, go, go, GO,' said Tom. He looked hard at his Granny.

'Did you run fast when you were little?' he said.

'Yes, I did,' said his Granny, 'but I was best at climbing trees.'

'I like going up,' said Tom, 'but not coming down.'

'It gets easier,' said his Granny, 'your arms grow stronger, you know.'

'One day,' said Tom, 'I'll swing like a monkey or Tarzan.' Then he made a Tarzan noise, and his Granny went POP.

When it was time to go home with his mother, Tom carried the big brown carrier bag.

'Can you manage?' said his mother.

'Of course he can,' said his Granny. 'His arms are stronger every day.'

But Tom knew and his Granny knew that the brown bag wasn't heavy at all.

As Tom and his mother walked to the bus stop all the people they passed thought, 'What a strong boy, carrying such a big bag.'

Then they met Mr Jones from next door.

'Hello, Tom,' said Mr Jones.

'Hello, Mr Jones,' said Tom, 'thank you for the matchboxes.'

'You're welcome,' said Mr Jones. 'I'll go on saving them for you.'

And Tom knew that Mr Jones knew that the big bag wasn't heavy at all.

When they got off the bus Tom said to his mother, 'One day I'll carry the shopping and my

cheek will be very tough. Then I'll go pop whenever I like.'

'Did you have a good walk?' said his mother.

'Granny had a good walk,' said Tom, 'and I had a good skip.'

Then he ran down his garden path with the big bag bumping his leg.

When Tom's mother opened the front door they could smell the baked potatoes. She squeezed the brown skins. 'Done,' she said, 'jacket potatoes.'

'Why not dressing-gowns?' said Tom.

'Or slippers?' said his mother. 'My feet are tired.'

'Or pyjamas?' said Tom. 'Can we have them again soon?'

'What?' said his mother. 'Pyjamas?'

'No,' said Tom, 'baked potatoes.'

'Yes,' said his mother, 'but potatoes are heavy, you know. You can carry the next bag home.'

'All right,' said Tom, 'and I'll make mud soup. Then I'll play with my matchboxes while the potatoes cook.'

'What are you going to make?' said his mother.

'I don't know yet,' said Tom, 'a farm perhaps, or a very long wall.'

He swallowed the last mouthful of potato. 'I'll practise going POP while I think.'

His mother made a loud pop.

'Like this?' she said.

Tom felt inside his cheek with one finger.

'Yes,' he said, 'like that.'

The
Bus Ticket

Jamie's big brother Donald went to school. Every school day Jamie and his mother went to meet him at the school gate.

'Is it time to go for Donald?' said Jamie.

'Yes,' said his mother and they set off.

They walked part of the way and then they caught a bus. Jamie liked walking to the bus stop. Just near their gate was a big red pillar box. Sometimes Jamie's mother said, 'Will you post this letter for me, please?' and Jamie said, 'Yes.'

Then she lifted him up because he couldn't quite reach the slot.

One day when they set off earlier than usual they saw a postman taking all the letters out of the pillar box and putting them in his floppy bag. Then they watched him drive off in his red van to the next pillar box.

'I'd like to be a postman,' said Jamie. 'I'd like to drive the van.'

'They don't all drive vans,' said his mother, 'some postmen walk about delivering letters. And what would you do about all the dogs in people's gardens?'

'I wouldn't touch them,' said Jamie, 'but I won't mind about dogs when I'm big. I don't mind them nearly as much as I used to.'

'That's true,' said his mother, 'and I don't mind cows, much.'

'When I'm a postman,' said Jamie, 'I'll take a special postman dog with me. He can carry the letters in his mouth.'

'Won't they get wet?' said his mother. 'Or he might eat them.'

'No,' said Jamie, 'he'll be very careful and good. He won't chew the letters at all or dribble. And everyone will say, "What a clever dog." Perhaps I'll let him wear my postman hat.'

Jamie's mother thought. 'Perhaps he'll have one of his own,' she said.

A little way past the pillar box they came to a seat for people with tired legs. Behind the seat was a lamp post. Donald was too big, but Jamie could just squeeze between the lamp post and the seat. Then came a low brick wall to drive along, brrm, brrm, and jump off. Then came the bus stop.

One day Donald was waiting for them at the school gate.

'You're late,' he said, 'I've been here ages.'

Donald was holding a big sheet of grey paper.

'Be careful,' he said, 'the paint's still wet.'

Donald often painted pictures of buses and fire engines, and Jamie thought they were lovely.

'We'll have to run for the bus,' said their mother, and Donald's new picture flapped as they ran. There was a queue of people waiting to get on so Jamie and Donald and their mother rushed up just before the bus moved.

'Fares' please,' said the conductor.

'One and a half, please,' said their mother in a puffed voice.

'That's right,' said the conductor, 'the other little boy doesn't need a ticket yet.'

When they got off the bus Donald said, 'I'm not a little boy. I go to school.'

But Jamie didn't say anything at all. He trudged along beside Donald and their mother. He didn't drive along the wall, brrm, brrm; he didn't squeeze between the lamp post and the seat. He sat down.

'My legs are tired,' he said, so Donald and his mother waited for a minute until his legs felt better. Then Jamie walked straight past the pillar box and in through the gate.

Their mother opened the door.

'I think there's a good story today,' she said. 'Could you switch the television on, please, Jamie?'

'All right,' said Jamie, then he sat on his stool and waited all by himself for the story to begin.

Donald went into the kitchen to talk to his mother.

'You know,' he said, 'I think Jamie is sad because he doesn't have a bus ticket.'

'You don't need a ticket until you're five,' said his mother.

'Well, I think he needs one now,' said Donald. 'And I'm going to make him one.'

So Donald's mother gave him a piece of postcard and Donald drew a red bus on it. It was a good double-decker bus with an upstairs and a down-stairs and a lot of windows. Then on the other side of the ticket he put numbers and writing, small and black and very careful. Then he gave it to Jamie.

'Thank you,' said Jamie.

Then he laughed at the story and ate rather a lot of egg sandwiches for tea.

The next day Donald went to school and at home time he looked out for Jamie and their mother.

'Have you got your ticket?' said Donald.

'Yes,' said Jamie. 'It's in my pocket.'

'I used to keep my bus fare in my glove,' said their mother. 'And sometimes it got stuck down a finger.'

'Mittens are better,' said Donald and the bus came.

They got on the bus: Donald first, then Jamie, then their mother. Donald and Jamie squashed together next to the window and their mother took up the rest of the seat.

The conductor said, 'Any more fares?'

Their mother said, 'One and a half, please.' Then he gave her two tickets, one blue and one white.

At the next stop an inspector got on. He wore a long green overcoat and a special smart cap. As he came down the bus between the seats he said, 'Tickets, please,' and 'Thank you,' when all the grown-ups and all the children held out their tickets for him to see. Then he said, 'Tickets, please,' again and Donald and Jamie's mother held out the two tickets, one blue and one white.

'Thank you,' said the inspector, then he saw Jamie's postcard ticket. 'Ah,' he said, 'yours is a season ticket, young man. You can use that for several days.'

Then the inspector punched a little hole in Jamie's ticket because it was special.

Donald and Jamie and their mother got off the bus at the next stop.

'Perhaps I'll be a bus inspector,' said Jamie, 'not a postman.'

Then he drove, brrm, brrm, along the wall. He squeezed between the lamp post and the seat.

'A bus driver might be better,' he said. 'I'll think about it.' Then he ran round the pillar box.

'There's a door in the pillar box,' he said, 'but no one lives there.'

Donald walked along with their mother.

'I'm glad the inspector came on the bus today,' she said. 'It was lovely Jamie had his own ticket.'

'Yes,' said Donald, 'I didn't know I'd made him a season ticket.'

Then he ran after Jamie. Jamie was turning round and round, 'I'm a helicopter,' he said and fell over.

'You crashed,' said Donald. 'I'm the fire engine,' and he rushed up sounding his siren.

But Jamie didn't cry. He just stood up and flew along with his arms out like an ordinary aeroplane.

The next day Donald was waiting for them at the school gate and they all ran for the bus.

'Fares, please,' said the conductor.

'One and a half, please,' said their mother and Jamie showed his postcard ticket. At their stop Donald got off the bus first, then their mother, then Jamie.

They walked as far as the seat, then just as Jamie

was squeezing in front of the lamp post Donald said, 'Have you got your ticket?'

'No,' said Jamie, 'I posted it in the little box like the other people when I got off the bus.'

'Oh dear,' said their mother, and Jamie stood quite still behind the seat.

'It's all right,' said Donald, 'I'll make you a new one for Monday. I like drawing buses.'

'Thank you,' said Jamie, and he drove off, brrm, brrm.

'You'll be making tickets till the cows come home,' said their mother.

'What cows?' said Donald.

'Not real ones,' said his mother, 'it just means for a long time.'

'Only until he's five,' said Donald, and ran down their path.

Then he braked hard and parked in the space next to Jamie.

Treat Day

It was not a good day. It was cold and Jane's mother had a headache. Jane was tired of being quiet.

Then there was a ring at the door and it was her mother's friend Mrs Morgan.

'Could you come for a walk?' asked Mrs Morgan. 'I feel fat. I need a walk, but I don't want to go by myself.'

Jane looked hard at Mrs Morgan. Jane thought she wasn't that fat, but you couldn't tell really because of her thick coat and scarf.

'Well, I can't really come out,' said Jane's mother.

'Well, could Jane come with me instead?' said her friend.

'Would you like to, Jane?' asked Jane's mother.

Jane thought. It wasn't much fun staying at home with a headache, even if it wasn't your head-ache.

'Would you be lonely?' she asked.

'No, I'll go to sleep,' said her mother.

'Yes, please, I'd like to come,' said Jane and ran to get her coat.

'You'll need a scarf too,' said Mrs Morgan.

They set off. Mrs Morgan was not as tall as Jane's mother so it was a change to be with her. When Jane climbed on the low wall and walked along holding her hand, she was almost as tall as Mrs Morgan.

They decided to go to the park to feed the ducks – if the ducks were out on such a cold day.

It was all right. They could see the ducks, tiny, swimming in the distance – and there was one drake with a shiny green head. Jane threw the bits of old bread for the ducks. One crust landed on the bank, not in the water. The drake left it alone. Why didn't he want it? It was easy to climb out of the water, even for a duck (or a drake).

'Perhaps he's choosy,' said Jane. 'I don't like cauliflower; perhaps he doesn't like my old bread. What does a duck have for a treat?' asked Jane.

'I don't know,' said Mrs Morgan. 'Perhaps a juicy worm?'

'What does a worm have for a treat?'

'I don't know really. Perhaps a soggy old leaf?'

'What does a cow have?'

'Long green grass and NO buttercups.'

'What does an elephant?'

'Hay, I should think, and a bun on her birthday.'

'What does a cat have?'

'A saucer of cream and a place near the fire, though I knew a town cat once who liked old sandwiches and potato crisps.'

'What does a dog like?'

'A fine juicy bone and somewhere to hide it.'

'What does a hen like?'

'Corn in a corner and dry dust to bathe in.'

'What does a bear like?'

'Plenty of honey and NO bees. What do THREE BEARS like?' asked Mrs Morgan.

'Porridge and porridge and porridge!' said Jane. 'What do *you* like?'

'Toast and tea all ready for me,' said Mrs Morgan and they began to walk home.

They walked home the other way. This was a special treat way – better for children than for grown-ups. You could walk under a bridge and shout and the bridge shouted back. It was like looking in a mirror and seeing yourself, if you shouted under the bridge, your voice bounced back at you. Well, almost, anyway. Jane had a few turns and each time her voice bounced back.

'That,' said Mrs Morgan, 'is an echo.'

They turned the corner into Jane's street and went in through the big door of the flats. They only had to wait a minute for the lift, then up they went to the sixth floor. Jane rang her own doorbell, just like a visitor.

'Did you have a good walk?' asked Jane's mother. 'My headache's gone, so I made cinnamon toast to celebrate.'

And sure enough, Jane could smell the spicy sweet cinnamon and sugar toast.

'What a treat,' said Mrs Morgan. 'And it's not even my birthday.'

The New Joke

Sam liked jokes. Nearly every morning he put his empty egg-shell upside down in his Dad's egg-cup. Then he called his Dad.

'Breakfast is ready,' he said.

'I'm ready for my egg,' said his Dad.

Then he laughed because Sam had made him a trick egg. You couldn't tell from the outside that the egg-shell was empty. Sam laughed too, but he wished he could think of a new joke.

One wet day Sam wore his wellingtons to go round to his Grandad's. Sam walked in all the puddles; he turned back and splashed through the good ones again. His feet didn't get at all wet, but he didn't think of any jokes at all.

> Dr Foster went to Gloucester, [thought Sam],
> In a shower of rain.
> He stepped in a puddle
> Right up to his middle
> And never went there again.

But that was someone else's joke. Perhaps Grandad would help. He often thought of funny things.

'Hello, Grandad,' said Sam, 'I like wellingtons,' but he didn't like taking them off. He tried to push one boot off with his other foot. He hopped around making muddy marks on the floor, he got cross, he sat down and kicked, but still his boots wouldn't come off.

'I'll give you a pull,' said Grandad, and off came the boots. 'What you need is a boot-jack.'

Sam was surprised. 'I've got two boots already,' he said. He looked hard at his Grandad, 'And my name's Sam.'

'I know,' said Grandad, 'I've known you for years. I mean a boot-jack. It is a special wooden thing for pulling boots off. It's called a boot-jack.'

'Oh,' said Sam, 'I didn't know. What is it like?'

Grandad thought. 'Well,' he said, 'we could make one. I've got some scrap wood and it wouldn't take long. What time is your Mum coming for you?'

'Half-past four,' said Sam.

He could almost tell the time and he could remember times very well.

'Let's get busy then,' said Grandad.

Sam found a piece of plank a little longer than a shoe box.

'Will this do?' said Sam.

'Yes,' said Grandad, 'that will be fine.'

Grandad measured a little way from the end and made a pencil mark on the wood.

'Measure twice, cut once,' he said. 'Measure twice, cut once. Hold it firm, please, while I saw.'

Then Grandad cut a little pointed bit of plank with his saw.

'It's a mouth,' said Sam.

'It's for biting boots,' said his Grandad.

'No teeth,' said Sam, 'like a baby.'

'Or me,' said Grandad. 'My teeth only *look* real you know. Now you nail this other little bit underneath.'

Grandad held the nails firm with the pliers while Sam hammered. Sam did miss the nails once or twice, but he didn't hit his Grandad with the hammer.

'There you are,' said Grandad, 'there's your boot-jack. You can take it home with you. I'll make another to keep here.'

'Thank you very much,' said Sam. 'It will be good for rolling marbles down, but what about my boots?'

'Ah,' said Grandad, 'you put one foot uphill and let the boot-jack bite your other boot. Your foot will slip out of your boot before you know it.'

'Thank you very much,' said Sam. 'Can I take home the bit you cut out, please?'

'Yes,' said Grandad, 'you're welcome.'

When his Mum came at half-past four Sam showed her the boot-jack, but he kept the little cut out piece of wood in his pocket. When they got home, Sam put one foot uphill to hold the boot-jack steady, and it pulled his first boot off. Then he let it pull the second boot off too.

'Is that how it works?' said his mother. 'I've never seen one before.'

'Yes,' said Sam, 'it's quite easy. Grandad showed me.'

Then he went away by himself, mysteriously.

He hid the little cut out wedge of wood under his sweater to go upstairs. Then he got out his

paints. By the time he had finished painting the wood yellow all over, he was rather yellow himself. He put the wood in a secret place to dry, washed the paint brush and washed his hands. He wasn't always so careful and tidy, but this time he didn't want anyone to know he had been painting.

When his Dad came home for tea, there on the table, next to the butter was a fine piece of yellow cheese.

'That cheese looks good,' he said.

'Nothing I like better than a good slice of cheese,' said his Dad, as he tried to help himself.

'That's funny,' he said, 'this knife won't cut the cheese. I'll try another.'

But the next knife wasn't any better.

'Where did you buy this hard cheese?' he said to Sam's Mum.

'I didn't buy it,' she said. 'Sam must have brought it home from Grandad's.'

And Sam said, 'I didn't buy it: I made it.'

Then Sam showed his Mum and Dad how the pretend cheese fitted into the hole in the boot-jack.

'Look,' he said, 'it's a baby jigsaw with only two pieces,' and they laughed.

Then he put his boots on and pulled them off in

a second to show his Dad how the boot-jack worked.

'You needn't make a boot-dad and a boot-mum for your boots,' said Sam, 'you can borrow mine.'

'Thank you,' said Sam's Dad. 'Now what can we make for Grandad?'

'The pretend cheese will make him laugh,' said Sam.

'Good idea,' said Sam's Dad. 'What about some pretend bread?'

'You two!' said Sam's Mum. 'I'm going to make some scones.'

'My cheese ones?' said Sam.

'No,' said Sam's Mum, 'real ones.'

So Sam went to fetch the mixing bowl.

Bird Day

John couldn't go out to play because he had a cold. His mother gave him a square of chocolate.

'Be careful,' she said, 'I almost ate a piece of silver paper once by mistake and I thought my teeth were falling out.'

'Were they?' said John.

'Not really,' said his mother, 'I've still got them, all the better to eat things with – but it felt horrible.'

'I like silver paper,' said John.

'So do I,' said his mother, 'in the right place.'

John smoothed and smoothed his new silver paper until it was smooth as shining silk. Then he used it to turn an ordinary brown penny into a silver treasure one (not to spend in a shop, of course, but to keep in his secret box).

Although John had a snuffly nose, he didn't feel ill. He felt like being busy. He went for the button box and he took out his store of silver paper. Then he tipped the buttons out on a tray. He knew them all: the small pearly shirt buttons, the big silver

one the bus driver had given him, the black shiny
ones with metal stalks and the ordinary ones, not
very interesting by themselves, but good for
arranging. Then he found something he hadn't
seen before.

'What is this?' he said. 'It's brown, but it isn't
an ordinary penny.'

'No,' said his mother, 'it's a very old one called
a farthing. I put it in the button box to keep it safe.'

'It's got a bird on,' said John. 'Is it a robin?'

'No,' said his mother, 'it's a wren. It's brown all over and it makes a lot of noise for its size.'

John looked hard at the bird on the farthing.

'It's tail pokes up,' he said.

'Yes,' said his mother, 'and it hops very neatly. People call it Jenny Wren.'

'I expect they call the boys Johnny Wren,' said John.

He put a piece of silver paper on the farthing and pressed and pressed until a silver bird showed through. Then he covered the whole chocolate paper as a present for his Dad.

'I know,' said his mother, 'you can give the birds somewhere to live,' and she drew a big tree on ordinary paper.

John moved the farthing about under the tree paper and crayoned and crayoned until the tree was full of birds, high up and low down.

'Look,' he said, 'they live in flats.'

Then he gave the treeful of birds to his Mum for a present and yawned.

'Thank you,' she said. 'Are you sleepy? Why don't you have a nap?'

Now in John's house they had a special chair. It was like a bed and like a rocking chair at the same time. You could lie in it, or you could sit up and rock. When people didn't feel well they could sit in the chair and put their feet up and then they felt better. John's mother put his sleeping bag in the chair and John snuggled down in it.

'I feel better,' he said, but he closed his eyes all the same. The next minute he was fast asleep, dreaming of silver things.

When he woke up he could smell cooking.

'Biscuits,' he said. His mother had baked biscuits without him. He jumped out to the kitchen in his sleeping bag, feeling cross. He didn't feel any better when his mother laughed.

'Are you having a sack race?' she said.

'No,' said John, 'and *I* cut the biscuits out.'

'I did it for a surprise,' said his mother, and John saw the rows of duck-shaped biscuits cooling on the tray.

'You know what,' said his mother, 'next time you could paint the heads green with my food colour, then we'd have duck and *drake* biscuits.'

'Yes, I'd like that,' said John, and he walked out of his sleeping bag.

Then he remembered.

'I had a dream,' he said.

97

'What about?' said his mother.

'I was skating on a silver pond like people on television,' said John, 'and there was a swan with baby swans on her back.'

'Was the mother swan skating too?'

'No,' said John, 'she was watching me. Her wings were all tucked up so the babies didn't fall off.'

'Did you fall over?' said his mother.

'No,' said John, 'I kept my arms out and went very fast.'

'That was clever,' said his mother, 'and you got back in time for tea. Did you get hungry skating?'

'Yes,' said John, and he began to set the table.

He put the silver bird paper on his Dad's plate and the treeful of birds on his Mum's. Then he put some plain silver paper on a saucer and set a duck biscuit to swim on it. The table looked lovely.

John's Dad was very surprised when he came home.

'Goodness,' he said, 'did I forget? Is it someone's birthday?'

'No,' said John's Mum. 'It's John's bird day.'

'Oh,' said John's Dad, 'Happy Bird Day, John,

and thank you very much for my silver bird day present.'

Then they all had tea and John said, 'Next time we have a bird day I'll paint some drake biscuits, or I might try a swan.'

He bit the head off another duck biscuit.

'Swans have black feet,' he said, 'and drakes have green heads. It's nice they're different.'

Carrot Tops

Neal looked at the wet grey roof opposite.

'I wish we had a garden,' he said.

'Well, you could make a little one, if you like,' said his mother.

'How little?' said Neal.

'As little as a saucer,' said his mother.

'I can't play in a saucer,' said Neal.

'No, but you can play *with* one.'

Neal was interested in spite of himself. Half of him wanted to be cross, but the other half wanted to know about the saucer.

'Which saucer?' he said.

'That thick old blue one,' said his mother. 'I think it's on the draining-board.'

'I can remember,' said Neal. 'I think I can remember when I couldn't reach the draining-board. It's funny I grow and things don't.'

'Trees do,' said his mother. 'You could grow some tiny ones.'

Neal found the saucer and waited for the next thing.

'Carrots for dinner,' said his mother.

'I'll cut the tops off, then you can plant them. Find some little stones from our holiday and you'll have a saucer garden.'

'Carrot tops aren't interesting,' said Neal.

'You wait,' said his mother.

Neal chose some good stones to go with the carrot tops, then he watered them all. He only poured a little water because a saucer doesn't hold much. (The water slops out so easily.)

'Look,' he said, 'the stones look different when they're wet, but they go all pale again when they dry.'

'You could put some in a jar of water,' said his mother, 'and see if they stay the same.'

'All right,' said Neal.

'They may smell a bit funny after a day or two,' said his mother, 'but you can always change the water.'

'They won't grow,' said Neal, 'and the carrots only look like left over dinner.'

Every day Neal looked to see if the carrots had water. They drank it up, but not when Neal was looking. Then on the fourth day they sprouted tiny, fresh green shoots.

'Look,' said Neal, 'they think they're in a

garden. Will they grow bottoms as well as tops?'

'I don't think so,' said his mother, 'but the tops will be good.'

Neal felt a little pleased with his saucer now, so he carried it into the front room and put it on the windowsill.

'They need light,' he said.

Every day the carrot top ferns grew a little bigger.

'They are like little trees after all,' he said. 'Jungle trees.'

He arranged his plastic animals all round the saucer.

'Look,' he said, 'they're drinking at the jungle pool.'

If he half shut his eyes and put his head close to the windowsill, the animals looked quite real and the carrot tops quite jungly. He was staring at the animals, to keep them real, when he saw someone staring back at him. It wasn't an animal, well, not a plastic one: it was a human, a boy as big as Neal looking in through the window.

'Oh,' said Neal. 'Hello.'

'Who's there?' called his mother from the kitchen.

'I don't know,' said Neal.

There was a knock at the door and there stood a woman and a boy.

'Hello,' said the woman, 'you must be Neal. I used to play with your mother when we were little. This is Stephen.'

Neal's mother came in from the kitchen drying her hands.

'Hello,' she said, 'how lovely to see you. Hello Stephen.'

'I knew you must live here by the carrot garden,' said Stephen's mother. 'I forgot the number of your house, so Stephen and I have been all down the other side looking for clues.'

Neal and Stephen arranged the animals in a long procession on the lines in the carpet.

'They've had their drink,' said Stephen.

Then they put the animals in the carpet circles.

'They're safe in sheep pens now,' said Neal.

Stephen liked the wet stones.

'Can I put my marble with your stones?' he said.

'Yes,' said Neal.

'You can bring it back when you come to my house,' said Stephen.

'All right,' said Neal.

'Tell you what,' said Stephen, 'I'll put a carrot garden on our step, then you'll know it's my house.'

'All right,' said Neal, 'but tell me the number in case the carrots don't grow.'

'It's number six,' said Stephen. 'Number Six, Carrot Top Gardens.'

And Neal laughed.

The
Balaclava Helmet

One cold morning the postman brought a small brown parcel.

'Look,' said Hugh's mother, 'it's addressed to you, "Hugh Jones, 1 Hollyshaw Lane".'

'Yes,' said Hugh, 'Hugh Jones, 1 Hollyshaw Lane.'

'Aren't you going to open it?' said his mother.

'Yes,' said Hugh, and he did.

Inside the brown paper was some white tissue paper, and inside the white tissue paper was a red woollen something, a red woollen something with two holes.

'What is it?' said Hugh.

'It's a Balaclava helmet,' said his mother. 'It's a kind of hat Granny's knitted to keep your ears warm. Why don't you try it on?'

Hugh put on the Balaclava helmet.

'I can't see anything,' he said in a red woollen voice and his little brother David laughed.

'The hole goes in front,' said their mother, 'then you can look out.'

'Like an owl,' said Hugh, but he put the helmet on back to front again to make David laugh.

'I wish Granny could see you all dressed up,' said his mother. Then she had an idea.

'If Mrs Boulton will look after David tomorrow, you and I can go into town together.'

The next day Hugh put on his blue coat and his brown lace-up shoes. Then he put his Balaclava helmet on back to front.

'Where's David?' he said in his red woollen voice.

David usually screamed and kicked until all the zips on his snowsuit were done up, but this time he was too busy laughing at Hugh.

'That was quick,' said their mother. 'We can catch the early bus.'

They pushed David in his pushchair round to Mrs Boulton, then they looked both ways and crossed the road to the bus stop.

When the bus came they went upstairs. They sat downstairs if they had David and the pushchair to manage. That day they were lucky: the upstairs front seat was empty so all the way to town Hugh and his mother looked out over the high walls and the fences. Hugh looked at other people's back gardens and he watched the traffic lights.

'Red, orange, green,' he said. Then he pressed hard with his feet to make the bus start again.

They went past the library and past the market. Then they got off the bus at the railway station.

'I don't like coming downstairs in a bus,' said Hugh. 'I'm glad our house keeps still.'

It was cold and draughty in the railway station, but Hugh's ears felt warm in his new Balaclava helmet. He thought of his old snowsuit.

'Did I scream like David?' he said.

'Sometimes,' said his mother, 'but you soon forgot.'

As they went along Hugh was so busy looking up at the high roof that he almost walked into a bucket of water. A man was scrubbing the tiles with a machine, so Hugh and his mother tried not to walk on the clean part. Hugh said to the man, 'Your machine is leaving a soapy snail trail.'

His mother looked at the little brushes whizzing round and round. 'I think it's a set of energetic hedgehogs,' she said.

'Hedgehogs or snails,' said the man, 'I'd rather them than me.'

Hugh and his mother walked away past the bookstall, and then they walked past the ticket office with its queue of people waiting to buy tickets. Then Hugh looked up towards the roof again.

'That's a funny place for a television,' he said,

'and what a dull programme, all numbers and writing.'

'It's interesting when you can read,' said his mother.

'What does it say?' said Hugh.

'It tells you where all the trains go and which platform you need.'

'Are we catching a train?' asked Hugh.

'No,' said his mother. 'We can't today, but we're doing something else instead.'

They walked on a little way then his mother stopped.

'Here we are,' she said.

They were standing outside a stall like a solid looking Wendy House. There was a curtain over the top half, but Hugh could see a big mushroom stool inside.

'What's it for?' he said.

'It's a machine for taking photographs,' said his mother. 'We can't see Granny for ages, so we're going to send her your photograph.'

Hugh looked at the outside of the stall and sure enough it was covered with photographs of people: some with hats and some without – but no one had a Balaclava helmet.

'Perhaps I'm the only one,' said Hugh.

He sat on the stool then his mother turned it round and round until he was high enough for the camera to see him. Then she put twenty pence in the machine.

After a little wait a green light went on, there was a sudden flash and a click.

'I'm a spaceman,' said Hugh. 'Is that all?'

'Not yet,' said his mother. 'You have three more turns.'

Three times the green light shone and three times the flash made Hugh jump. Then it was over.

'Let's wait outside,' said his mother. 'The photographs will come out of that slot.'

While they were waiting a policeman strolled up, very tall in his stiff black helmet.

'Hello,' he said, 'what's your name?'

'Hugh Jones,' said Hugh. '1 Hollyshaw Lane.'

'It's good to know where you live,' said the policeman.

'Would your helmet fit in a photograph?' said Hugh.

'Yes,' said the policeman, 'I'd turn the stool round and round and sit lower down. But there'd be more helmet and less me.'

'Yes,' said Hugh, 'I see.'

'I'll tell you something else,' said the policeman, 'when I was a little boy, I thought policemen had big heads to match their helmets. But now I know they don't.'

'I know,' said Hugh, 'but my head's the same size as my helmet.'

'Yes,' said the policeman, 'it's a good fit. I'd

like a Balaclava for cold days but I have to wear my uniform helmet.'

There was a click and four photographs in a row came out of the slot.

'Like stamps,' thought Hugh, 'with my head instead of the Queen's.'

'I must be off now,' said the policeman. 'Goodbye, Hugh,' and he walked away with long steps past the bookstall.

'Let's go home,' said Hugh and they hurried to the bus stop. Their steps weren't as long as the policeman's, but they went faster. This time they stayed downstairs on the bus, but Hugh sat next to the window.

They went to fetch David from Mrs Boulton.

'Has he been good?' asked their mother.

'Of course he has,' said Mrs Boulton.

Hugh thought that David wasn't at all good sometimes, but he didn't say so.

When they got home Hugh's mother took a pair of scissors and cut the row of photographs into four separate ones.

One for Granny.

One to put in the book with all the other photographs.

One to put on the mantelpiece.

'What about the other one?' said Hugh.

'You'll see,' said his mother.

When Hugh's Dad came home he saw the new photograph on the mantelpiece.

'I'd like a new Balaclava Hugh to put in my wallet,' he said. 'Is there a spare one for me?'

'Yes, there is,' said Hugh's mother, 'and we could even take some of David in his snowsuit.'

He'd scream, thought Hugh. Then he looked at himself in the photograph again. He leant against his Dad's knee.

'Did you know,' he said, 'did you know, Dad, that policemen's heads aren't nearly as big as their helmets?'

'I know now,' said his Dad, 'but I thought they were, when I was little.'

The
Jumble Sale

Ruth looked at the hand-painted notice on the church door.

'What does it say?' she said.

'Jumble Sale,' said her mother. 'And that part with the letters all squashed together says, "Saturday, 2 pm". Saturday is a longer word than they thought.'

'Can we go?' said Ruth.

'I should think so,' said her mother. 'We might find some bargains. I bought my little wooden box at a jumble sale.'

'How much was it?' said Ruth.

'1p but that was a long time ago.'

On Saturday afternoon Ruth and her mother were waiting in a queue for the Jumble Sale to begin. Ruth looked at the cobwebs in the corners of the window.

'Why was Miss Muffet so frightened?' she said. 'I like spiders.'

'I know,' said her mother, 'but if there came a big slug, would you give it a hug?'

'No, I would not,' said Ruth, 'but I don't mind snails.'

'I didn't like the dark much when I was little,' said her mother, 'but I grew out of it.'

'Like shoes?' said Ruth.

'Yes,' said her mother, 'like shoes.'

'Grandad's horse wouldn't walk past a wheel-barrow,' said Ruth.

'I know,' said her mother, 'and we had a parrot who hated hairbrushes.'

'What was the parrot called?' said Ruth.

'Polly,' said her mother.

'Polly put the kettle on,' said Ruth.

The door opened and everyone surged in. Some-one trod on Ruth's foot, but it only hurt for a moment.

'Meet you at the dress stall,' said her mother.

'All right,' said Ruth, but she hoped to find a little wooden box for 1p first.

Then she saw it – not a box, but a dress, a black lacy dress, light as a cobweb.

'How much is it?' asked Ruth, but no one heard. You have to speak up if you're not very big. Ruth tried again.

'How much is this dress?' she shouted.

'Goodness,' said the lady behind the stall, '20p.'

'Oh,' said Ruth, 'I've only got 5p.'

'Well, I really can't let it go for less,' said the lady, 'look at the lace.'

Ruth looked at the lace, then she wandered away to the other end of the hall. She watched the people

rummaging through the piles of clothes. She looked at the row of pointed shoes.

'Witches,' she thought, 'I could see if there are any books or comics.'

Then she saw the yellow wallpaper.

'How much is it?' she asked, and this lady heard the first time.

'Let me see,' she said, 'would 1p a roll be all right? Three rolls would be 3p.'

'Yes, please,' said Ruth, and she carried the wallpaper away.

Her mother was talking to a friend so Ruth went to stand near the dress stall. The Jumble Sale was nearly over so there wouldn't be long to wait. Then she saw it. The black dress was still there. Could she ask again? The lady might say, 'Go away, I told you already,' or 'You are a nuisance.'

'I'm not frightened,' thought Ruth and she stepped forward.

'How much is the black dress, please?' she asked firmly and politely.

'Well,' said the lady, 'no one else seems to want it. You can have it for 2p now. It's a bargain.'

'Thank you,' said Ruth and ran to show her mother.

'Oh, lovely,' said her mother. 'I'm glad you were lucky. I didn't find any bargains today.'

Then Ruth remembered the wallpaper propped against the wall.

'Three rolls for 3p,' she said.

'You are kind,' said her mother, 'it's just what we need for the kitchen.'

Ruth's mother turned to her friend.

'Look what Ruth's bought. Can you come home with us to celebrate?'

'I'd love to,' said the friend.

So they walked home together; then they all had tea.

Tony's Day Out

Tony often stayed with his Granny until his Mummy came home, but one day he walked with his Granny to the bus stop. First he practised standing on one leg, then he practised standing on the other, then he watched the sparrows having a bath in a puddle. He talked very quietly, not to frighten the sparrows. Then WHOOSH, along came the bus and the sparrows flew off in a hurry.

'Hello, Tony,' said the bus driver.

'Hello, Dad,' said Tony.

And he climbed the big steps by himself, went along between the seats and sat next to the window. The bus conductress pressed the bell, Tony waved his Granny good-bye and they were off.

'Ouf,' went the seat as a large lady sat down next to him.

'You're very young to go on a bus by yourself,' she said.

'No, I'm not,' said Tony.

'Fares, please,' said the conductress. 'No, he isn't too young, because he isn't really by himself.'

'That's my Mummy,' said Tony and they smiled
at each other.

The large lady paid her fare and Tony's Mummy
counted the change and smiled at her too.

When the bus drove into the bus station all the

people hurried away. Tony got off too, but he waited. His Dad backed the bus slowly into its place in the row of buses; it squeezed in among the others until you couldn't tell it was special. Tony waited again while his Dad wound a little handle round and round until a new set of writing came in the little window on the front of the bus. Now everyone could tell where the bus was going next time it went out.

But Tony and his Mummy and his Dad weren't going on a bus yet. They walked to the canteen where the bus drivers and conductors and conductresses had cups of tea. Tony thought he must be the only person with no dark green uniform and no silver badge, but one man called out, 'I see you have a new bus crew today.'

And his Dad said, 'Yes, it's grand to have company.' And he carried their tray to a table. They had two cups of tea and one glass of orange squash. Well, it wasn't really a glass, it was a paper cup.

As the drivers passed they said, 'Hello, a new driver,' or 'Hope they all paid their fares on your bus.'

Tony wanted to say something too, but he

couldn't think of anything, so he smiled and took care not to spill his orange squash.

Then it was time to do the shopping. Everybody seemed to have the same idea. Once Tony bumped into a shopping bag, or a shopping bag bumped into Tony, but it only hurt for a minute.

'Oranges, five for 10p.'

'Tomatoes, they're lovely, rock hard tomatoes.'

All the stall holders were shouting at the tops of their voices.

Suddenly Tony thought of something to say.

'Tomatoes,' he shouted, 'buy my tomatoes.'

And his Mummy jumped because he shouted so loudly and she wasn't expecting it.

'You like a job, son?' asked the stall holder.

'Not today, thank you,' said Tony and they walked around the market, choosing the best tomatoes and the best oranges from the shining piles. Tony thought the stalls were like shops having a picnic.

Tony carried the potatoes, he didn't carry the eggs in case they broke, and he didn't carry the tomatoes in case they squashed (even though he had shouted about them). Just when the potatoes were getting heavy, there was the bus station. And

there was the bus with the name of Tony's village showing in the little window at the front. Tony climbed on the bus again – but this time he wasn't by himself at all. His Mummy and his Dad got on too – they were all passengers together.

His Dad said, 'It's nice to look at the country instead of the cars.'

His Mummy said, 'It's nice to forget about the fares.'

Tony said, 'It's nice to go home together.'

And he sat next to the window.